Where is Molly's Teddy?

written by Jay Dale

illustrated by Katy Jackson

Molly saw Little Sam in the garden.

She saw him playing with her teddy.

"Little Sam," said Molly.
"That is **my** teddy."

"No! No! No!" said Little Sam,
and he ran from the garden.

Molly saw Little Sam go into the house. She saw him go into her room.

Molly looked for Little Sam,
but he ran out of her room.

Molly went from room to room, but she did not see him.

Molly went into Little Sam's room. She saw him, but she did not see her teddy.

"Where is my teddy?" said Molly.

But Little Sam ran from his room.

"Mum!" shouted Molly.
"Little Sam is running
from room to room.
He saw me and he ran.
Where is my teddy?"

"Little Sam," said Mum.

"Come here."

But Little Sam ran into Molly's room.

Mum saw him go.

"Where is Molly's teddy?" she said.

"It is her teddy.

It is **not** your teddy."

Little Sam went to the big box, and out came Molly's teddy.

TOYS

15

"Good boy," said Mum.

But Little Sam ran into the garden.